Pete
Stays
Home
CW00867524

Questions to discuss with your child after reading *Pete Stays Home*

- How does Pete feel when he realises he won't be able to see his friends or his grandparents?
- How do Pete's feelings about the cave change?
- How do you think Pete feels about his time spent at home with his mum?
- What are the different feelings Pete experiences when he is able to go outside again?
- Why might Pete feel nervous about going outside again?
- Can you think of two words to describe what it is like when Pete is able to go outside again?
- How does Pete feel when he sees his friends and grandparents again for the first time?

Pete Stays Home

by Karra McFarlane

Illustrated by Kim Hankinson

In a beautiful lush forest
full of trees,
where all played together,
the bears and the bees,

there lived a young bear,
his friends called him Pete.
He was gentle and friendly,
and full of mischief.

Pete lived with his mum
in a big cozy cave.
Pete loved his mum,
she was caring and brave.

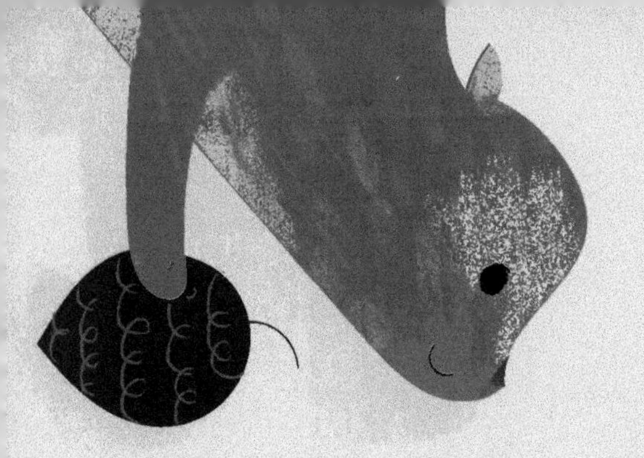

Pete was a sociable,
popular bear.
He had lots of friends
and he loved to share.

Pete and his friends played
day after day.
He thought the fun times
were here to stay.

But then, suddenly,
the sun began to disappear.
And the birds in the trees,
Pete could no longer hear.

Pete's mum arrived
to collect him from school.
Time to go home
to their cave, big and cool.

"Winter is coming,"
she said to Pete.
"When the snow falls thick,
we must retreat."

"We must be patient
and hide away,

until the sun
shines bright – another day."

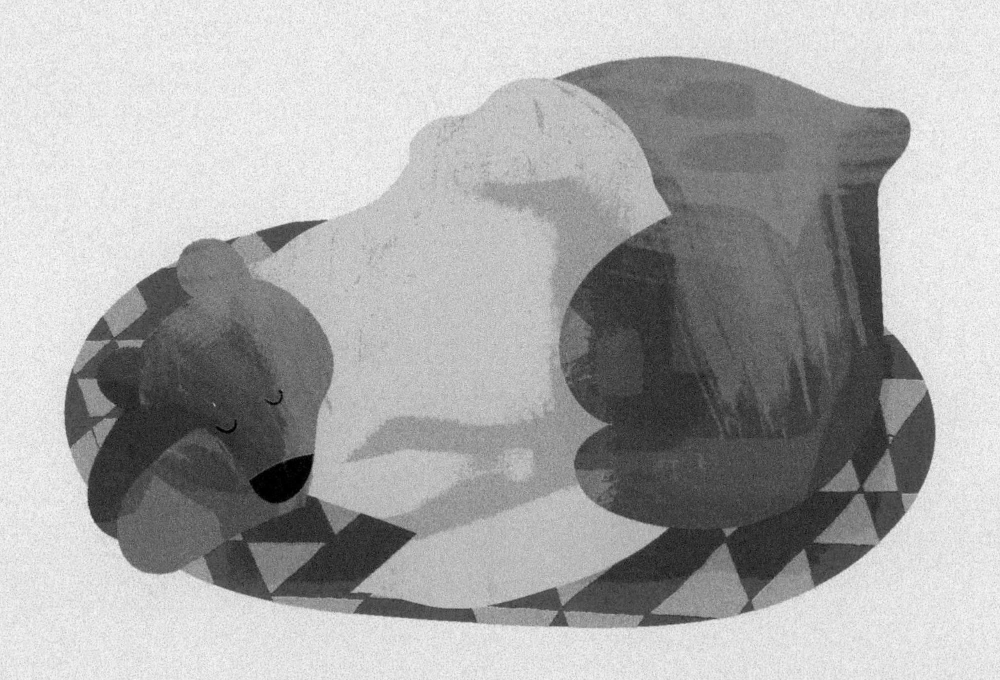

Pete felt sad
and all alone.
He didn't want to
stay at home.

"I want to jump, and run
and play.
I can't stay in this cave
all day."

"I want to see Nan and Gramp!"
said Pete.
"My time with them
is such a treat."

"Nan and Gramp must stay at home,
safe and warm.
They will not make it through
a big swirling storm."

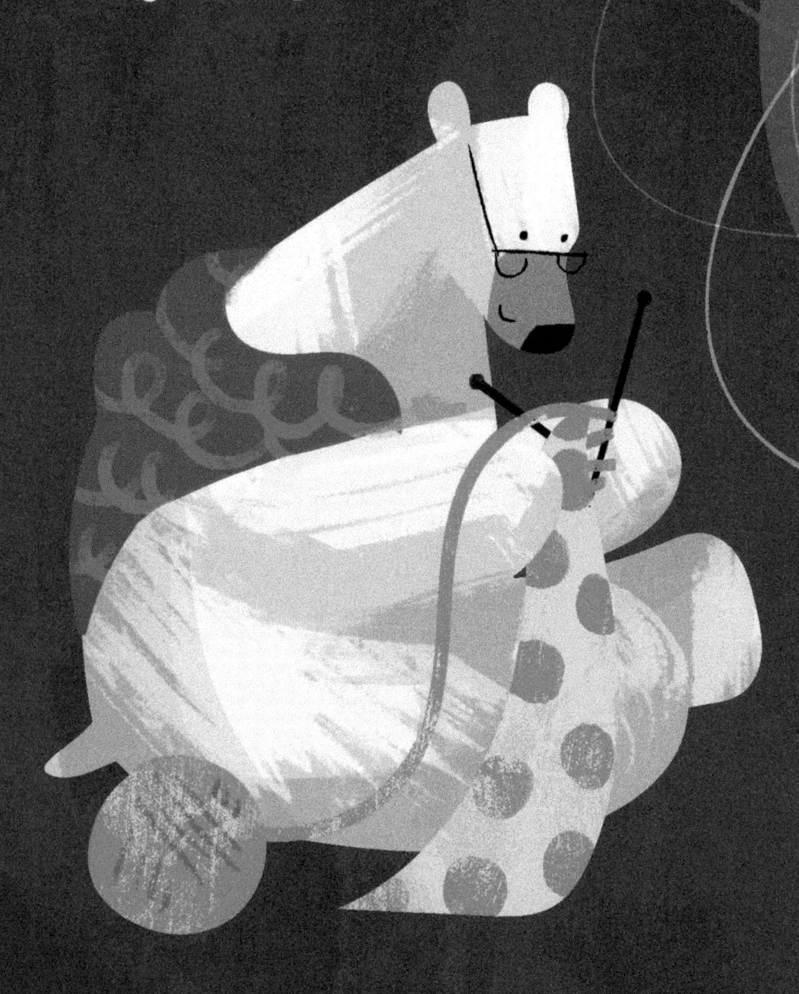

For the long days, weeks and months
that passed,
Pete and his mum stayed in
and did crafts.

As time went by, the big cool cave
felt cozy and safe.
Pete and his mum filled it with
love, fun and cakes.

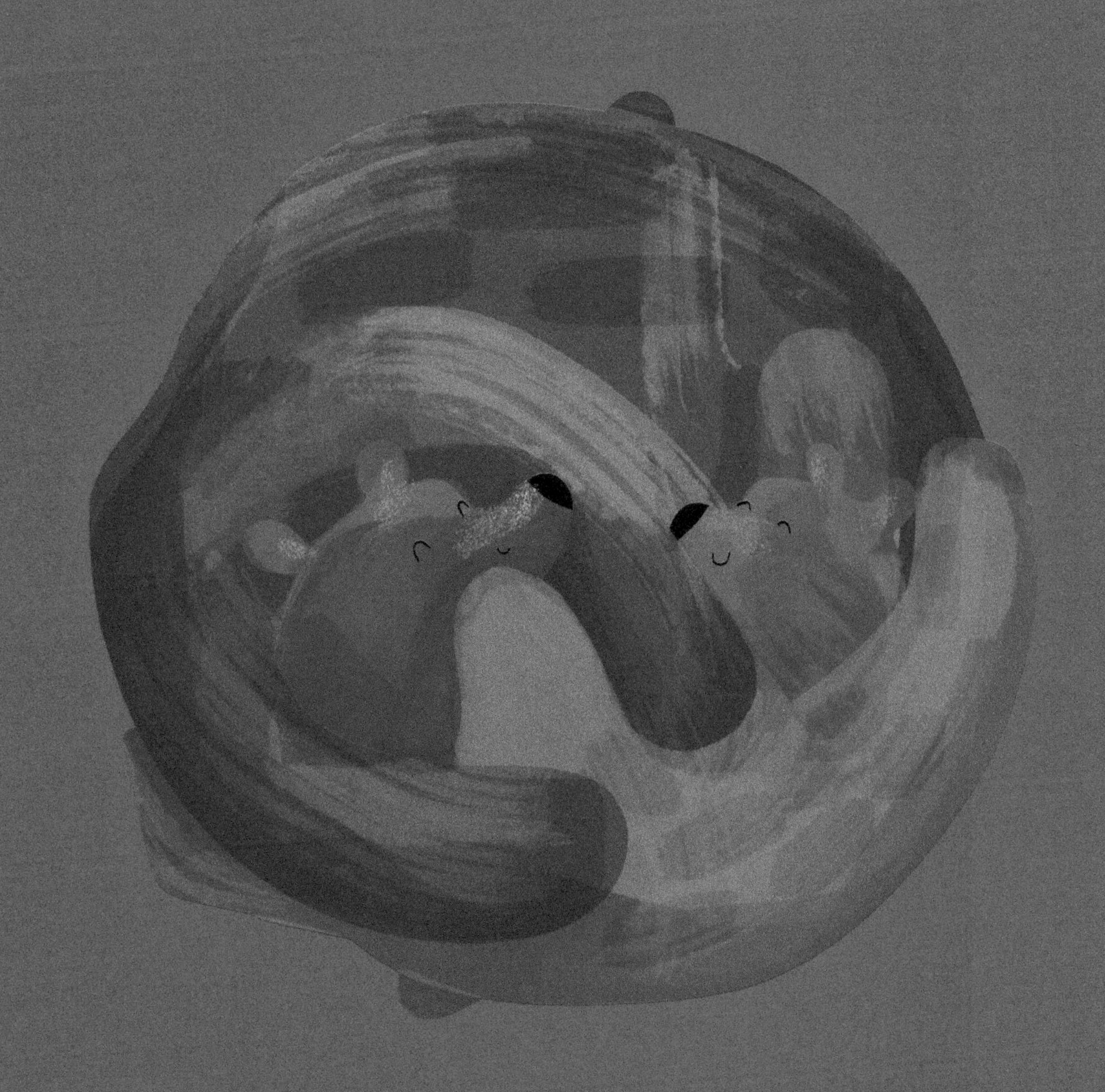

They played, they laughed
and they stuck together.
They stayed inside,
they rode out the weather.

Pete missed his good friends,
he missed his school,
but knew one day
he would see them all.

When the time to leave
finally arrived,
Pete could not
hide his excitement inside.

He would see his friends,
his Nan and Gramp.
He could not wait to
run, jump and stamp.

But when the time came
to step outside,
he felt a butterfly
tickle inside.

What would it be like
in the world he once knew?
Would it be different?
Would it all be new?

Pete stepped outside
on tippity-toes.
He looked up and breathed in,
twitching his nose.

He smelled the sweet flowers,
he sniffed the fresh grass,
his time in the cave
was now in the past.

He looked around
and was happy to see
all of his friends
jumping with glee.

His Nan and his Gramp
gave him a cuddle.

Pete was content
in their big cozy huddle.

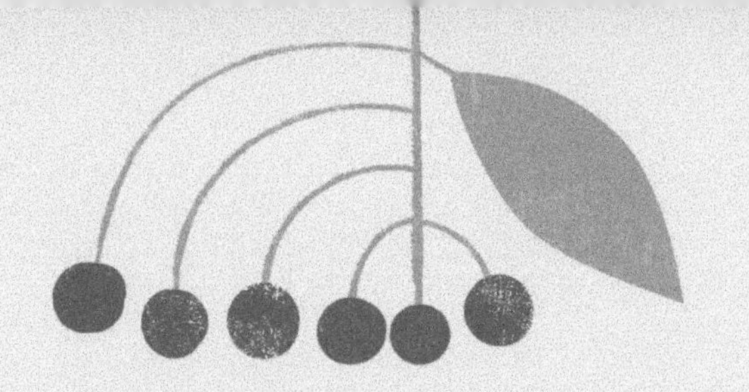

Although times were hard,
although it was tough.
Pete was happy
they had all done enough.

They had ridden out winter
and made it through.
With all they had done,
the time – it just flew!

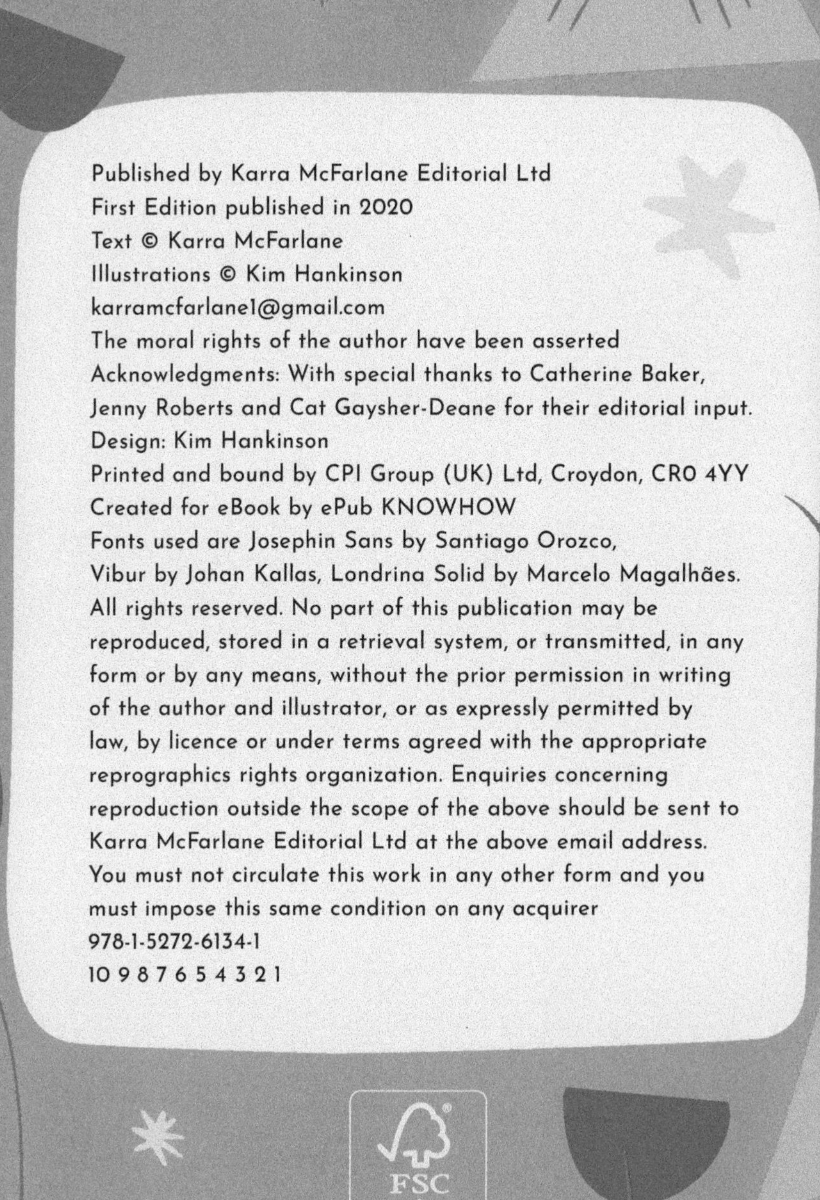

Published by Karra McFarlane Editorial Ltd
First Edition published in 2020

karramcfarlane1@gmail.com

Acknowledgments: With special thanks to Catherine Baker, Jenny Roberts and Cat Gaysher-Deane for their editorial input.
Design: Kim Hankinson
Printed and bound by CPI Group (UK) Ltd, Croydon, CR0 4YY
Created for eBook by ePub KNOWHOW
Fonts used are Josephin Sans by Santiago Orozco, Vibur by Johan Kallas, Londrina Solid by Marcelo Magalhães.

978-1-5272-6134-1
10 9 8 7 6 5 4 3 2 1